Catalina Ghost Stories

Jim Musgrave

Published by EMRE Publishing, LLC, 2022.

This is a work of fiction. Similarities to real people, places, or events are entirely coincidental.

CATALINA GHOST STORIES

First edition. July 14, 2022.

Copyright © 2022 Jim Musgrave.

ISBN: 979-8215683750

Written by Jim Musgrave.

Table of Contents

Catalina Ghost Stories

By
James R. Musgrave
© 2012 by James R. Musgrave
ISBN 979-8215683750
Published by EMRE Publishing, LLC

These stories are works of fiction. Names, characters, places and incidents are the product of the author's imagination, except for historical characters, or are used fictitiously, and any resemblance to actual persons, living or dead, events, or locales is entirely coincidental.

Contemporary Instructional Concepts Publishers is a publishing house based in San Diego, California. Website: emrepublishing.com
For more information, please contact:
EMRE Publishing, San Diego, 92120
publisher@emrepublishing.com

Cover and book design by EMRE Publishing

Interactive and Multimedia Enhanced eBooks

EMRE Publishing is now selling completely "enhanced" versions of its books, including *Catalina Ghost Stories*, through the unique Embellisher Multimedia Stream platform. Simply register inside the eReader to have access to the variety of titles. They contain relevant historical videos, music, interactive content, and a complete audiobook edition in many of the great titles.

Natalie Wood's death has just been re-opened by the Los Angeles Police Department. What does Natalie's ghost have to say? You'll find out by reading "Natasha and the Captain," a story that uses information gathered at the scene by eyewitnesses and used in this story.

"Pearl Zane Grey" tells the story of how the famous writer of Westerns became trapped in the afterlife on Catalina, pursued by his nemesis and cowboy actor, Tom Mix. How these two must compete will give you a new vision of the afterlife.

Lewis Hack Wilson was a victim of the new "dead ball" in 1931. Did this cause him to haunt the club house on Catalina where the Cubbies held Spring Training for many years? Find out in "The Dead Ball."

In "The Somnambulist," the real-life murder of 41-year-old Marie Weinfurtner is given a strange twist. What if her 25-year-old boyfriend were innocent? This story shows what could happen if someone were able to kill in one's sleep.

Finally, the story "Kafka and the Chewing Gum Man" is a surrealist exploration in bad karma and how ghosts can redeem themselves in the absurdity of our world.

Natasha and the Captain

YES, I WAS NATASHA when my father Nick gave us the new names in San Francisco. But I come from Russian royalty, so my real name, according to Maria, my mother, was Natalia Nikolaevna Zacharenko. My mother was right about so many things. How do I begin to explain?

First off, I am now dead, and this is probably the biggest role I've ever had. You see, I am an actress, and the Hollywood studios gave me the actress's name of Natalie Wood. I've never liked that name. It's so stark and inflexible. People joke about it. For example, when I first returned to Santa Catalina in my present form, the tourists were asking, "What kind of wood doesn't float?" The answer, of course, was "Natalie Wood." Also, people are always knocking on wood to ward off bad luck. Friends, who were a bit drunk at cocktail parties, would knock on my head whenever talking about their future trips or physical ailments. "We'll be going to the south of France in June, knock on wood," they would say, and I would get their knuckles on my head. Thus, you can see why I don't like the Hollywood name they gave me.

Now, back to mother. She is the genius. I didn't understand her when I was older, but when I was younger, and now that I am dead, I see how right she really was! She used to tell us we were from royalty—the Romanoff's no less—and we had to escape the Bolshevik murderers who were slaughtering the wealthy by the thousands during the revolution. Or she would tell people, we were from gypsies in Barnaul, southern Siberia. "We have magic potions and my daughter, Natasha, she is the most mysterious creature of all! She knows the secret to life itself!" I believed her then when she said it. So, when she told me at the movie theater in Santa Rosa, California that the big newsreel camera pointing at us from the screen was "taking my picture for all America to see," I would smile and make googly faces to attract attention.

My mother, bless her, packed the whole family up, and we moved to Los Angeles when Hollywood director Irving Pichel took a liking to me on a shoot in Santa Rosa and "wanted to adopt me." I had a screen test, and my first acting role came at age five. The great artist and director, Orson Welles, said I was a born professional. "She's so good, she's terrifying," was what he really said. I just thought I was always in front of that camera my mother showed me in the movie theater, and I suppose that's why I was so terrifyingly good. In my later years, I suppose I just became a bit terrifying, but in a far different way.

We are the best liars in the world, we actors. Of course, I suppose the writers of stories and screenplays come in a close second, but if you examine the whole concept of acting, you'll see that making believe you are somebody else, which requires getting into the very person of that character and becoming him or her in so many ways that the person looking at you from the audience believes you *are* that other person! Mother was a liar like that, and so was I. However, now that I am a spirit, I find I have lost my motivation. Without our bodies, we actors are not worth much.

Therefore, I can see you putting the facts I have told you together in your mind as you read this. She was a born liar, and her mother lied to get her into acting, and she became one of the most respected liars in the business of Hollywood. What do you suppose frightens a lying actor more than anything in the world? Why, the truth, of course. The truth that you get old, and your breasts sag, and you lose your star figure, and that you will eventually have to play in B-movie horror roles the way Bette Davis and Joan Crawford did. I remember going into a showing of *What Ever Happened to Baby Jane?* starring those renowned women of the theater, and I came out crying my eyes out. They were reduced to these two figures of elderly pastiche, monsters of the Hollywood Midway, put on the screen for teenagers to gawk at and make fun of right inside that theater.

Let me tell you a truth we living dead must live with you can't remember what you did in your life. You heard me. I can recall everything any other actor on the planet did when I was alive, but as for me, no way! I can't remember acting in a single motion picture or TV commercial! We are, you see, just ordinary ghosts. We are here to haunt. We haunt this worldly plane to discover what caused us to die such mysterious deaths. Until we find out the truth (there's that ugly word again) about our deaths, we are forbidden to go beyond (whatever is beyond I really can't say as I am still doing this haunting gig on Catalina Island).

I have a dreaded fear of deep water. In fact, I never would go into my pool at our home in Beverly Hills. RJ knew that. He's my on-again, off-again (our little joke) husband, Robert Wagner, star of many TV shows, including *Hart to Hart* and *It Takes a Thief*. Now, however, in my spiritual state of existence, I can actually walk on water! It's true, and I'm doing it right now. I am walking on the water of Lover's Cove, and I'm heading for the tavern where I know a man is drinking, as this is the anniversary of my death, November 29th, and he has been coming back to the island of Santa Catalina from Florida for many years to pay his respects and to travel the places we traveled on the night I died. What better place to haunt? I can see the flying fish as they cascade in shimmering leaps above the waters in front of the boats that shine spotlights over their bows to attract these unique fish. I am heading to the Avalon Grille on Crescent. As I walk up and onto the land, I find it appropriately amusing that I can travel through the tourists who once were my fans. In my life, I was the ephemeral image they saw up on the screen, and they took me into their lives, and now I can enter their bodies with the same élan. As I enter a person, say this young man who has never even seen me act, an image of a woman will be thrust into his mind, perhaps when I was young, dark-haired, moody brown eyes, believing in the miracle of imagination to cure all ills, and he will smile, as he does this very moment, jerking the earplugs out of his ears, looking around, hoping to see the woman who matches the vision inside his head. But, I walk on down the street, passing through others, and they, too, become momentarily mesmerized, as if losing a train of thought because of an image I provoke in their psyches.

There's the restaurant up ahead. It's on the corner overlooking the tiny beach and the shore. I can see people inside, still drinking at the bar, and several couples are at tables. They stay open until past 1:30 AM, and it's now 10:00 PM. We dead haunt you living to find out information. The only hope we have is that you can give us clues to release us from this agonizing search for the truth. The skipper of the *Splendour* sits at the end of the bar, his drink in front of him, staring down into it as if it contains some answers he needs. He looks so much older now, thirty years later, and he has let himself go. Whereas I died in fine form of 120 pounds, he now has a gut, and he needs a shave, although he did sport a full beard in 1981, the last time I was with him. He once told me confidentially that he grew his beard because he always had acne scars, and he never wanted people to see his face. He was a kind and gentle man, and I love him dearly. However, I sense he's tortured by something in his past, and I believe it may lead me to my destiny in the afterlife.

Oh, yes, the "afterlife." Another trick we spirits have about which you may not be completely aware when we perform it on you is the ability, we must enter your mind and read your thoughts. This is what positive spirits do. The cursed spirits, or the spirits of those who were evil in their terrestrial lives, also enter your minds, but this becomes a "possession" of your mind, and psychiatrists often diagnose it as schizophrenia or some other personality disorder. The Bible had it right the first time: it's possession by an evil spirit.

When I entered this man's mind, I did not alter his thoughts one iota. He simply gave me what I came here to receive. The startling aspect to entering this man's consciousness was the fact that he was looking for me. I did not, however, recall his name, but the forces of my need brought me directly to him on this date, and we became one.

Natalie, if you can hear me, I want you to know that I'm doing it. After all these years, I'm going to clear your name and bring the truth out into the open. I've been so guilty all these years, but I've told it all to my good friend, and she's publishing the book America needs to know.

I became transfixed with what he was thinking. This was a man who knew what happened that night in 1981. I would follow him to the ends of the earth to find out what he knew. We swallowed the last of the drink, got up from the bar stool, and walked out onto the boardwalk of Crescent Avenue. The evening breeze was strong, just the way it was that night. We could feel (yes, when I enter a body, I can feel what he or she feels) the misty rain against our face, and he brushed his cheeks with his coat, a blue one, and he sneezed once. I saw we were walking to Metropole where most of the taxis were.

We got into a taxi and headed inland. I knew it was about a ten-minute drive from Avalon to Two Harbors, as I gradually remembered this man, and we traveled this route on that night. I didn't want to stay with RJ, as he had been angry about something, and I wanted to take the first boat or plane out the next morning. It was the off-season, however, and there was no transportation. He was looking out the window at the passing darkness, and he began to think again.

I stayed on board with RJ, Natalie. You and CW went to the restaurant. I kept telling him he should cancel this outing, that you were too upset, but he said, "Natalie will get her wish fulfilled, a full weekend with her co-star." He sounded revengeful, Nat, it's the truth, and his words were ominous. We joined you and CW at six, and we drank together in the bar until seven, when we were seated for dinner. CW and I went back in the dinghy to get more wine, two bottles of Soave Bolla. We left one bottle in the dinghy and took one bottle back to the restaurant. CW offered me a joint to share, and we smoked it while on board the Splendour.

The cab stopped at the Isthmus of Two Harbors, and we got out. The rain was coming down a bit harder, and he turned up his collar. All that he was thinking was beginning to stir something deep inside me. I couldn't understand what it was, at first, but as he began to think again, I tried to listen more carefully and comprehend his meaning. He walked down to the pier that jutted out into the waters. The yachts and small craft were moored there, just the way our *Splendour* was that night, rocking in the surf that was kicking up quite a bit of white froth. As he walked along the creaking boards, his thoughts began to bombard me like lightning bolts from the gloomy clouds that covered us.

The mood was tense at the dinner table that night at Doug's. We all had a few after-dinner drinks, but RJ wanted to get back to the boat. You wanted to socialize more, but we left about 10:15. The headlight on our rubber dinghy was broken, so I used the flashlight to guide us back to where we were anchored.

Yes! This was it. I was going to hear the truth at last about what happened that night. Death clouds your spiritual reality with its finality, and that's why you must search out the truth for yourself. I was becoming more anxious as we walked further down the pier and out into the water. The waves were coming up over the wood, and onto the skipper's feet, as the weather was getting increasingly stormy.

After you lit candles in the main salon, we opened the last bottle of champagne. You and CW began talking about how the life of the actor was like that of the gypsy. You must constantly be ready to pull up stakes and move to the next gig. It was an endless succession of doing your magic, moving on, and doing your magic again. That's when RJ picked up the bottle and smashed it against the bulkhead. RJ screamed at CW, "Do you want to fuck my wife, is that what you want?" To CW's credit, he just got up and returned to his cabin for the night. The glass was all over the salon, and nobody cleaned it up. I know how neat you were, Nat, and I'm sorry for that.

I started to see CW in my mind's eye. His large, hazel eyes were captivating on the set, and he put every ounce of himself into his roles. I was anxious to land a role like he had in *The Deer Hunter*. I didn't want to go down the road that Joan Crawford and Bette Davis took. I wanted one last chance at the Oscar. The movie we were doing together, a low-budget science fiction piece, certainly did not fit that bill, and I told CW and my husband so. CW was sympathetic, but RJ was angry. He was always accusing me of having affairs on the set with my leading men. I never did, when I was married, and this was well known amongst our crowd. We may be prima donnas and spoiled brats, but we were also like a small town. We knew what each other was doing. RJ wanted us to be alone in his world of controlled reality, and this boat, this *Splendour*, was symbolic of his need for that control over my life. I could see that now very clearly.

The skipper reached into his front shirt pocket and pulled out a marijuana joint. He lit it, inhaled deeply, and the thoughts became much more rapid, as if he wanted to get it all over with at long last.

You were so embarrassed, Natalie, you went directly to your cabin. He followed you, in hot pursuit, and I could hear the argument begin. It was so loud, I knocked on the door to see if I could calm down the situation, but RJ told me to not interfere and to get lost. I reluctantly went up to the bridge, directly above your stateroom. I then heard what sounded like things and possibly people hitting the bulkheads and things being thrown at the overhead. It was directly below where I stood, so how could I not hear it? Next, I saw you both on the open deck. You had carried your argument out there, and it was 11:00 PM, as I glanced at the bridge clock.

Argument? It was new to me, and yet it began to leak into my memory like a lanced boil, filling me with dread. Those arguments were always on the boat. This was where he was the king, and this was where he wanted me to be his total slave! It began, in the early years, like a sexual dalliance, and we would frequently end our rows with hot sex. But, as the years progressed, and he became increasingly more jealous of my leading men, I became more and more frightened of these arguments. The lightning around us began to strike, and I could feel the rain pelting his body in big drops now.

I turned on the radio and tried to drown out the noise of your argument, but it didn't work. This was the mother of all your arguments. I looked out the side window, and I saw you dressed in your flannel night gown—what you always called your "Granny gown." You continued to yell at each other, so I closed the door. I thought you might have gone back into the stateroom, but then I heard him yell, "Get off my fucking boat!" I was scared shitless, Nat, but I waited 15 minutes before I left the bridge to check on you. When I arrived on the rear open deck, RJ was the only one there.

The onrushing fury of this version of the truth hit me full force. I became cold and even more ephemeral. I wanted to dissolve into a pinprick of reality and disappear, but he continued his discourse.

He was sweaty, flushed, anxious and disheveled, Nat. He told me, "Natalie is missing" and asked me to search the yacht. He led me through the stateroom, which was a mess; it had been spotless when I secured the dinghy an hour earlier. I went to CW's cabin, and he was sleeping, and then to my stateroom forward, but it was empty. I met up with RJ in the wheelhouse, and that's when he told me the dinghy was missing. I immediately wanted to use the searchlight to look for you on the water, but he got angry and said, "We're not going to do that. We'll wait to see if she returns."

The deep and the dark water! That was the curse my mother got from the gypsy fortune teller. Death in the dark water! I can feel it now, all around me, pulling me down, freezing my blood and my very soul! This is what was missing from that night of horror. I was drowning out there and nobody heard me!

I knew you had never taken the dinghy out by yourself because of your fear of the water, and you didn't know how to operate it. RJ opened a bottle of Scotch, and, God help me, I drank with him. We waited for two hours before I could convince him to call somebody. He didn't call the Coast Guard or other professional help. He wanted to call the locals. So, in about another hour, the Harbormaster arrived and insisted he call the Coast Guard. That's when RJ said he didn't want to get his name out into the press until we found out what happened. What happened? What happened was that he knew you were out there in the water. A witness in a boat next to us heard your screams for help, Natalie! She also heard someone say they were coming to get you. She said she called the Coast Guard, but nobody came. What was happening? Were you cursed? Had life itself turned against you? That's all I could think about all these years!

The minutes were stretching into hours, as the skipper finished his tale, and I was becoming increasingly frightened. I was no longer a tiny spot of existence; I was growing much larger and more dangerous.

RJ only wanted things controlled. He told me to stay quiet about anything I knew, and that's what I did, God help me! All these years. The Coast Guard finally came, and they were angry we hadn't called them earlier. They found you face down in the water at 7:45 AM. Both RJ and CW were flown by helicopter to the mainland before the investigative detectives from Los Angeles arrived. I had to identify your body. Your face was still beautiful, and it has haunted me in my dreams! RJ got me an attorney, he got me a job as an actor, but I escaped his control and moved to Florida. I have never forgotten you. But RJ has never returned to Catalina in over 30 years. Me? Nat, I've been living this night in my mind for all those years, and I come out here to bare my soul. And now, my truth is in a book for the world to read.

I grab the red down jacket and put it on before I leap, or else I slip on the ladder, or was I pushed? Either way, I am in that water forever! Deep and dark, it surrounds me, and the rain comes down, and I feel heavy in that darkness. The wind and dark ocean pull me away from you. It is like the darkness in the theater when the only light is the magic up there on the screen. My image is up there, for you all to look at. Darkness is your friend, but it is not my friend. But the light is coming. It is piercing my reality, and I begin to see those co-workers around me. Jimmy Dean holding my head as he cries about his cowardly father. Steve McQueen holding my hand as he walks me home to my big Italian tenement family. I can see you out there, my audience, my family, feeling for me, wanting me to learn my lesson so they can pretend life is fair and just and worth all of the pain. I see all my friends now, as clearly as the light that is now shining on us as we stand at the end of the pier on Two Harbors.

"Hey, buddy! You okay?" the voice from the Harbormaster came to us from over the waves.

I left the body of the captain then, and I felt exhausted with relief. The motion of the waves seemed comforting now, and the truth may be close at hand. The skipper of the *Splendour* nodded to the voice, as if it contained the humanity, he had been searching for all these years. "Yeah, sure. Thanks for asking. I'm heading back now."

Pearl Zane Grey

WHEN I WAS ALIVE, I hated reality. Now that I am dead, I understand what I missed. My father was a dentist in Zanesville, Ohio. Do you know what my childhood was like? I was a "Zane," and this meant the entire town watched me like a hawk circling above a prairie dog. My mother also named me Pearl to go with Gray, because we were English, and Queen Victoria's favorite color was pearl gray. My father changed our name to "Grey" because it was the British spelling of the color. I had to fight many schoolyard toughs over my first name, so I never used it when I left home.

I was taught the dental practice by my father, and I was pulling teeth (we called this process an "extraction" to sound aloof from that pulsing, swollen cheek reality in front of us) before I was twelve. Dad used to put the patient out with ether and call me in. I stood there as he demonstrated how to use the ivory handled tooth key from Chevalier of New York. It worked like a door key. A metal claw at the end of the key was placed over the tooth, and then my father twisted the handle. "It's all in the wrist, Son," he said. However, when I tried it the first time, I broke the tooth and fractured the patient's jaw. My father beat me and sent me to bed without dinner.

I remember one other time he beat me when I was fifteen. I had just written my first complete short story, "Jim of the Cave," about a kid who prefers to live inside a cave rather than go to school, and my father tore it up in front of my face and then beat me harder than I had ever been beaten before. He told me, "Life is real hard. You can't dream your way out of it!" I guess the sole purpose in my life after that day my father beat me was to prove him wrong. I was able to dream my way out of the insides of people's mouths, with their bad breath and their caries; I beat the hell out of other boys because I wanted them to feel what I felt at home.

Until I met Muddy Miser, I guess I was probably doomed to a life of criminality like the outlaws in the news stories. I loved playing pool, and I liked watching the tough guys strut around the table like they owned the world. Cigars, toothpicks, cigarettes and booze. That's what I thought my future held and then I met Muddy.

Muddy was an old man who told me to believe in my imagination. He said, "Z, there's a world out there filled with adventures. The men who founded this country never knew what to expect. They had to imagine it first. Take Melville and his white whale. Captain Ahab imagined that Moby Dick was his personal demon because the giant beast once took his leg. He wouldn't rest until he could fight that monster again. The idea that Moby Dick was roaming free out there in the ocean made him a crazed captain who was finally destroyed by his obsessive idea made flesh. So, you can't let one idea make you crazy, boy. I like what Henry Thoreau said. You must first build your castles in the air, but then you need to put the real foundations under them down here on earth."

Muddy taught me to fish and to follow my imaginary worlds wherever they led me. He told me to read Robinson Crusoe by Defoe and the *Leatherstocking Tales* by Fennimore Cooper. I also read dime novels that featured Buffalo Bill and Deadwood Dick. My biggest influence was a book about the history of the Ohio frontier called Our Western Border.

In my life as a writer, I wrote over 90 books, many of them published after I died in Altadena, California at the age of 67. I met my wife Dolly when she was 17, and with her help over the years, I made over a million dollars in my lifetime. In exchange for keeping my family intact, she received half of everything I made. In return, I was able to live my life as I saw fit. Lina Roth, better known to me as Dolly, knew about my father's beatings and my vow to live free, letting my imagination take me wherever it wanted to go. She agreed to help me with my passions. However, the only passion she fought me on the most was my passion for women. Finally, she gave in, and we were married in 1905, and we took off for a honeymoon at the Grand Canyon in Arizona. It was this passion for women which led to my present state as a ghost. Women were, for all intents and purposes, my white whale. I believe having to service all those women eventually wore out my heart.

When I wrote, I wrote in a fever. I could go many months without writing a word of my novels. However, I did keep a journal of my travels and experiences, and I also wrote down the conversations I had with my fellow adventurers. Then, when I returned to Dolly, I would write my invented stories enthralled in my reverie. My travels over the oceans, and through the deserts and canyons, were food from my subconscious that fed my literary world. Hundreds of thousands of words would pour forth from me during these months of creativity.

In my writer's world, I was free to feed all of my passions. My mistresses would come into my study to partake of my many manly virtues, and Dolly and I agreed to have the room closed off from the rest of the house. She would work on our business matters in her section, and I would partake of any wild desires I needed to fuel my stories of the Wild West. I would even take Dolly's young female cousins with me on my fishing trips to appease my passions during the lull between fighting huge marlins and gigantic sharks.

Why did I need strange women to quench my thirst for carnality? I suppose it was the same reason I needed to fish, to explore, and why I wanted to play baseball. When one fishes, one uses a "pole" with a "reel" on it. However, these manufactured tools mean nothing if you don't know which bait to use on the hook and what kind of noble fish you want to catch. When one travels in the wilderness, one has the tools by which to traverse: a horse, a tent and blanket, and some cooking utensils. However, once again, the journey is meaningless unless your mind is set on the proper reverence for what you experience. Yes, and to compete in baseball, especially as a pitcher, as I was, one must know how each tool is used: the bat is meant to strike the ball hard; the pitcher must learn to grip, spin and propel the ball towards the batter. However, without knowing each batter and how he swings at pitched balls, one will never be able to throw the exact pitch that will get that individual batter out. All batters are not equal, all adventures are not the same, and all fish are not identically caught. So, too, are women subject to an individual mastery that requires a monumental effort of learning to choose the right person to go after in the first place and the proper bait to lure them into your den.

Thus, my successes with my mistresses made me a master seducer. I knew the best candidates were either teenage women who had yet to learn about the world and its glorious possibilities, or widowed women, who had already experienced life and who had the wisdom of appreciating the act of gentle love for its own physical sake.

In fact, I kept a private journal that was coded in my own cryptography, and in it I described, in step-by-step detail, how one seduces a woman both physically and mentally. I also included many photos of my conquests over my sixty years on this good planet, and these photos allowed me to record each woman and her passionate position for posterity. It is this book that leads me to my present unholy predicament in my deathly state.

Here are the present rules of my spirit world. For, as you may have guessed, one does not escape the demons of one's earthly existence unless one can conquer his demons completely—even after death. When I lived, I described my demon as a hyena lying in ambush—that is my black spell! I conquered one mood only to fall prey to the next...I wandered about like a lost soul or a man who was conscious of imminent death. Therefore, as in my life, so it is in my death. I am not free to explore the world and enjoy its wild nature. No, I must protect my present world on Catalina Island from my arch-nemesis, and antagonistic evil hyena spirit, Tom Mix!

In life, Tom Mix made more money than I did, and he starred in many of the films made from my books. He was also a deserter from the military, and he was married five times to five different women! He even made money from a radio show that used his name and persona, but he never spoke or wrote one word. He grew up, like me, in Pennsylvania, but his was the State College section and not the Ivy League section where I went to college. He was a fraud and a circus act, and he used his own sister to practice his knife-throwing tricks. He did learn to ride and rope on a cattle ranch, and he was darned good at it, but in 1905, he rode in Teddy Roosevelt's inaugural parade with some rough riders from the Spanish War. Years later, his Hollywood publicists made it look like he rode with Roosevelt's Rough Riders, when, in fact, he was a deserter! Because of his homespun imitation of a cowboy, he was able to earn $10,000 a week for Fox Studios, at the height of the Depression, when other stars like Gene Autry, Randolph Scott and John Wayne were making $500 from other studios.

However, what made Tom Mix my real enemy was the fact that he became the President of the Tuna Club on Catalina Island, and he had a home built just below mine, where I had to look out my pueblo window every day and gaze down at that ghastly "M" emblazoned in crimson paint on his roof or surrounded in blinking lights every night! He was, in fact, a traveling circus and sideshow, all rolled into one man!

In life, we were both gone most of the year—me on my authentic fishing and traveling expeditions—he on his circus trips and phony western movie acting escapades. Every time his movie acting would hit the skids, or he or his wife of the moment would spend all the money, he would make his escape in one of the many circus shows around the country, where he would ride around a circus ring, on his "wonder horse" Tony, feeding the phony applause from his adoring fans who were just as crazy as he was. They paid him even more—$20,000 per week—to do this circus charade!

Finally, Tom Mix died in Arizona, at age 60, speeding down Route 79 in his 1937 Cord 812 Phaeton, with all his circus earnings inside a polished aluminum suitcase in the back seat. Was it irony when his vehicle came to a stop from its 80 miles per hour speed, this valise filled with gold and jewels flew up and hit him in the back of the head, killing him instantly? There was no other scratch on him, so I think so!

In the spirit world, God, Nature, karma, or whatever force it is that creates this reality, has placed me head-to-head against Tom Mix on Catalina Island. Once again, he is the President of the Tuna Club—as he was in real life—and, once again, I must confront him to gain any sense of freedom. We are both playing opposing roles in this parallel reality.

We ghosts live right beside you people in the "real world." In other words, we exist in our own dimension, and you exist in yours. Only those amongst you who have the extra sensory perception can see us from the other side—your side—but we spirits are still here. The rules of our reality allow us to touch, smell, taste, and hear other ghosts, but we can never kill each other because we are already dead. However, we can stop each other from doing things in our plane of life, and that's why Tom and I are pitted against each other.

It's just the way I saw things in my westerns. I am the free-spirited adventurer, armed with my weapon of intuitive genius, who keeps my cache of liberated women in (where else?) Lover's Cove. My women are, paradoxically, both women and fish. I suppose this is karmic justice for the two great passions I had in life. Yes, I must protect my harem of Mermaids from the sea nymph-rustling clutches of Tom Mix. The Fates have punished me by making these women fish from the waist down, so I can no longer partake of their treasures down below, but I can still appreciate their human forms above the surface, so to speak. Even though they are part fish, they are still flesh-and-blood beings, and I must protect them with all my spirit's cunning and guile.

At any rate, it is Tom's job to attempt to "mix" my herd of lovely mermaids in with that collection of circus freaks he has now assembled on the other side of the island. I've been over there, and he has Chinese boys joined together at the hips and shoulders and a woman who looks like a penguin. He has a man with skin dropping off and covering his face, and another "pony boy" who must walk around on his hands and feet with midgets riding him. The strangest freak I saw is the "octo man," who has three legs, four arms, four breasts with a small head and ear growing out of his stomach. There are even more freaks of nature there, but I became too nauseated to look at them all.

If Tom accomplishes this feat of thievery, he plans to place my girls with these other freaks inside the Wrigley Casino. He wants to show my fish maidens off inside giant saltwater tanks, along with these other monstrosities, to the gawking ghostly tourists.

I can see him now, portraying Jim Lassiter, the Mormon killer, my famous anti-hero in my most famous novel, *Riders of the Purple Sage*. He's riding on his ghost wonder horse, Tony, dressed in all black—Stetson, chaps, shirt, neckerchief, and bullwhips on either side of his midnight saddle. Guns are useless in our reality, as the bullets would go clean through me like mice through cheese. The whips, however, can tear into my outer particles of visible spirit flesh; I can feel the pain, and I can be stopped long enough for him to make a run at my water nymphs.

In a cloud of sand from the beach, he pulls up on his noble steed. Tony snorts and rears up on his hind legs, Tom smiling down at me like the Cheshire Cat. "Hey, Pearl! Aint'cha afeared you'll catch cold away from your cozy pueblo? Ya can't risk damagin' those delicate writer's hands, now can ya?"

I suppose Tom wouldn't be a very good villain if he didn't know every button to push on my dial of personality. So, I just play along with him. "What brings you down to this side of the island, Tom? Can't you find enough freaks for your sideshow? Have you looked in the mirror lately? Oh, I forgot. We can't look in mirrors—we're ghosts. If you could, however, you'd see one freak of a fellow staring back at you."

Tom, who was a constant fidgeter in life, kept circling his horse around me, in mincing steps, and tossing his reins from one side of Tony's mane to the other. "I heard you got you some new whores to play with, out in that cove yonder," he said, pointing like an Indian, with a broad wave of his hand, toward Lover's Cove. "Maybe they can change the name of the cove to Whoremaster's Cove, you reckon?" Mix smiled, flashing those false teeth of his that had to replace the ones he lost from his frequent falls and accidents while drunk.

"Say, how did you keep your wives straight? I guess they all spent your money because you kept them so happy under the covers, am I right? I heard you loved your horse more than your wives!" I took some enjoyment out of the frown that came over his face at that moment.

Mix pulled a long lariat from his saddle bag and began circling it lazily over his head. I could hear it swishing in the air, and it became larger in circumference with each revolution and draw from his rope. I tried to run down the boardwalk to get to the cove, but he was after me, racing along at a gallop on Tony. He finally reached me; his rope circled my body particles, and he drew his horse up and pulled tightly on the rope, bringing me down like a spring calf. As he walked toward me, I could see that famous grin again, and I knew he felt satisfied he had me.

"Oh, I'm sorry, Pearl. Were you going out to angle for one of them fish ladies in the pond? You can't catch many fishies with that little pole of yourn, little fella! Here, let me tie you up, so's you can watch a real man herd those finny heifers."

Tom Mix proceeded to bulldog me down to the ground and tie me up, quick as you please. I felt like I was in a surreal rodeo. "You just stay here, while I mosey out onto the pond to get me some fishy women!"

I watched, as Mix walked over to his horse and reached into his saddle bag again. He pulled out a big net and carried it purposefully down to the water's edge. I smiled, as I watched him struggle with the net, as he tried casting it over the waters of the cove. Once, twice, three times he failed to get the net high enough and wide enough to catch anything. Finally, with a big grunt, he was able to sling the big net out far enough, and it began to drop down into the salt water. Then, as he felt the weight of something inside, he walked back to Tony and tied an end of the net rope to the saddle horn and ordered his horse to pull. Tony, noble steed that he was, began prancing backward, pulling the net tightly up from the deep water.

Finally, I could see he had captured one of my mermaids, Jane, and she was enclosed inside the net like a Jack mackerel. Her beautiful blonde hair was wet and wild with the sea foam, but it was smashed down by the netting. Her wonderfully perfect face was also squished into a repulsive grimace, as were those exquisite breasts, which were heaving in the excitement of the capture.

Mix walked up to her and put his hand out to touch her inside the net. "Now, now, little gal. I ain't gonna hurt ya none. You're gonna be the star in my little show at the casino down the road."

Suddenly, I could see a flash of sunlight as it glanced off the knife in her hand. Just as in life, I always looked out for my women! Each one of my mermaids had her own knife. I have collected them from my many travels around the world. I gave a special knife for each one of my girls, and she promised me she would protect herself from any sea shark or land shark that would try to accost her.

In a few deft slices, Jane tore through the netting and pushed out into the water. All Tom Mix could see was her huge flapping tail as it sprayed water all over his black outfit.

As she was doing this, I was also cutting through the rope with my own knife that I had secretly stashed inside the cuff of my shirt. I stood up and shook the sand off my body. "I guess you have a lot to learn about fishing and women, my friend," I said.

Tom was so angry he was spitting as he climbed back on Tony. "You ain't never gonna fish these waters again, Pearl! I ain't finished with you yet! I'll be back, partner, quicker than the flick of a deer's tail. I'll get you and your Moby Whores if it's the last thing I ever do!"

I watched, with some satisfaction, as Tom Mix rode down Crescent, his horse passing through real life tourists and ghost tourists, without a care in the world, on his way back to his freak show inside Wrigley's Casino. I was certain he would return for another go at it, as this was our reality until the Gods of Fate were finished with us, and we could move on.

I looked back at Lover's Cove, and, sure enough, all of my girls were poking their heads up out of the water to smile at me! Fifteen smiling women, the same women I had in your real world, but now they were sea damsels, their hair shining in the sun, their eyes misty with gratitude. I know each one, her desires and her hopes, and her secret passions. With this knowledge, I will confront any Tom Mix out there, and I am certain I will prevail. The secret to life and death is out there in the waves, in the beyond, in the canyons and in the wilderness of nature. The lure of the sea is some strange magic that makes men love what they fear. The solitude of the desert is more intimate than that of the sea. Death on the shifting barren sands seems less insupportable to the imagination than death out on the boundless ocean, in the awful, windy emptiness. Man's bones yearn for dust. As for me, I prefer the sea!

The Dead Ball

WHEN WE PRACTICED BASEBALL on Catalina Island in 1931, we all knew the live ball was going to be a thing of the past. With the entire National League averaging .300, during the 1930 season, it didn't take a genius to know something had to be done. We all knew what would happen, but one man made it his personal vendetta to show his displeasure, and that man was the one who most benefitted from the harder apple. That man was legendary centerfielder and RBI machine, Lewis Hack Wilson.

I am telling this story because both Hack and I were born in Pennsylvania, but I was a college boy who was replaced by Hack when he arrived from the New York minor league team. I have been his backup replacement ever since. This is my story because I was the one who saw what happened on Catalina Island that spring of 1931, when the new ball was introduced to us.

Mr. Wrigley had his big house up on the hill, and he would often make rookies or other guys who had bad days on the ball field climb all the way up to his mansion and pay their respects by doing 100 pushups in his parlor. I'll tell you straight out that attendance at games was down a lot ever since the crash of '29. Fans just couldn't afford to pay the bucks, even if hitters were hitting over .300 and smacking 56 homers (like Hack did in 1930). So, the owners and the other officials of baseball got together in one of them smoke-filled hotels and decided to tone it down a little and cut costs, so to speak.

Now Hack, he was making the most of any player in the league, over $33,000 for the year, and everyone knew it. A backup replacement like me was lucky to clear $5,000, even though I had the most years on the Cubs, which were nine. I and Gabby Hartnett had seniority, but of course Gabby, being catcher, got a lot more money than guys like me on the bench.

On the day it happened, we had been on the island for a couple of weeks already, and Hack had been drunk at least five times. When that old steel mill worker, with the barrel chest and the flatiron face, gets a toot on, he's like a changed man. I know what alcohol can do to a man because of Hack, and most of the worst of my story was caused by demon rum.

We were living with Prohibition laws, but Hack had his way with Joe McCarthy, the manager. Spring training was when Joe let Hack have one night of "hootin' 'n hollerin'" each week, even though Hack reported to camp 20 pounds overweight.

We didn't play any big-league teams out on Catalina because it was too far for the travel, so we mostly played ourselves. Once in a blue moon we would play the Pacific Coast League Los Angeles Angels because they were close by, and Mr. Wrigley would send one of his steam ships over to pick them up and take them out to our digs.

It was on a night before we were to play the Angels that Mr. Wrigley brought out the guy who was going to explain the new ball to us. He was a runty litter bugger with horn-rimmed spectacles and little tufts of red hair that circled his pate like a ring of fire. Mr. Wrigley introduced us to him. "Boys, this is Charles Meriwether. He's going to explain the new ball we'll be using in the National League this season. The American League won't have the rubber around the cork center, just the raised seams. Otherwise, we'll be playing with the same ball."

Hack and Charley Grimm, our first baseman, were sitting in the back, and they were both pretty tanked up. When the little guy began his pitch, I knew something was going to happen, and it wasn't to be a pretty sight. The little guy had brought with him a baseball cut in half, and he showed us how the rubber was wrapped around "the pill" as we like to call the cork center. He also explained that the outside of the baseball was going to have raised seams, which would allow the pitcher to get a better grip on the ball.

"You better get a grip, Mister," we heard the voice coming from the back row. "You think I made my money because I was hitting a dead baseball? This here's nothing but a fix by the owners to keep us down!"

Mr. Wrigley was getting fidgety in his seat. He was a good old guy, and he really cared more about his players than most of the owners in both leagues, but even he would only put up with so much back-talk. He was also a strict Prohibitionist, and Joe McCarthy always had to protect Hack and a few other guys from his wrath.

Little Red Charlie started to explain again that this ball would be safer for fielders because it would be easier to field with the seams raised and the concussion subdued by the rubber inside and the thick horsehide on the outside. That's when Grimm made his famous horse laugh. He was raised on a farm, and he could make every sound any farm animal ever made since Noah's Ark. The guys started to laugh, and I even chuckled.

The little guy turned red in the face, however, and he picked up his two ball halves and stood up to go. Hack then threw the soft tomato at him and hit him on the back of his red hair tufts, spreading a crimson blotch of mushed tomato all over the back of his suit jacket. The guys laughed harder, but old Mr. Wrigley got angry.

"Wilson! I want to see you in my quarters tomorrow morning at eight!" Both Joe McCarthy and Rogers Hornsby, who were co-managers that year, nodded gravely at Hack, and he knew they all meant business.

WHEN HACK RETURNED to practice from visiting Mr. Wrigley's mansion, he had a weird look on his steely face. His eighteen-inch neck was still red, and he looked ready to spit fire at anybody who looked at him crossways. "Heathcote!" he yelled at me. "Get your damned glove. I want to warm up!"

At five feet six inches tall, with his size six shoes, people thought Hack couldn't get around much in the outfield. They were mistaken. However, he did make two big errors in the 1929 World Series against the Athletics, and fans would throw lemons at him during the 1930 season, even though that was his record-setting 56 home runs and 191 runs batted in that year. Hack even attacked a fan in the stands and caused a near riot.

When Wilson lost those two in the sun in the fourth game of the 1929 World Series, a kid came up to manager Joe McCarthy after the game and asked for a ball. McCarthy told the kid that all he needed to do was stand behind Hack in the outfield and he'd get plenty of balls.

That day Hack started throwing the ball at me, and as I could see he was angry, I was ready for what happened. He started steaming the ball into me after about five throws, until I dropped my glove on the grass and shouted at him, "Hey, Hack! I'm not Mr. Wrigley."

Hack just turned away from me and trotted back to the club house. We wouldn't see him until the following day.

What happened in batting practice surprised us all. The balls we had were not behaving like the new dead balls were supposed to. In fact, they were scorching the infield when hit like they were golf balls. I thought they might set the grass on fire. Then, big as you please, Hack got up to the plate to hit his practice pitches. I have never seen balls hit so hard in my entire career in the majors. Sure, I was in the 26-23 high-scoring game, when I got 5 hits and the Cubs won, but the ball that was being struck that day on Catalina Island was much livelier than any ball I ever hit. I was playing center when Hack was up.

Let me explain something. The Inn on Mt. Ida, which was Mr. Wrigley's mansion, was over 380 feet from where we played baseball. Mr. Wrigley liked to watch his players practice from his big picture window. However, since this distance was basically a vertical climb to the top where the Wrigleys could also see most of Avalon and Lover's Cove, it was not a true 380 feet in baseball distance terms. No, to hit a ball that high and that hard, the distance would have to be increased to about 580 feet, at least.

Only that's how high Lewis Hack Wilson hit one of those lively balls that day. I heard the crack of the bat, I saw the arc of the ball, and I just turned around and looked up into the distance where Mr. Wrigley's mansion stood. The ball kept going up, up, and up, until we all heard the smashing sound of glass breaking. It was a miraculous achievement, even with the balls Hack had substituted that morning. The Hack man had broken the owner's vista grande front window!

Lucky for Hack, Mr. and Mrs. Wrigley were down in town that day, and they were able to fix the window before they came back up to Mt. Ada. We all kept hitting those balls, and Hack was laughing and joking like a big old kid.

MY STORY GETS A LITTLE dark from here on out, so bear with me. The dead ball took its toll on many players in 1931 but none more so than Hack Wilson. It was basically the end of the Hack Wilson era. And, in a touch of irony, it was also the end of Cliff Heathcote's time on the Cubs.

Hack was in a slump in 1931, and he was benched in late May, and I took over his spot in center. Mr. Wrigley said he wanted to trade Hack in August after Wilson got into a fight in a club car with a sportswriter who gave him the ribbing over his 1929 errors in the fourth game. He kept shouting at the kid and pounding his face to mush, "It was that dead ball that did me in, you screwball, don't ya know nothin'?"

Hack had one more good season with the Brooklyn team, but he was out of baseball completely at 35 after a season of "A" ball with the Albany Senators. He lost all his money on bad investments, and he knocked around the country and ended up in Maryland.

Me? I had one 1929 World Series at bat with the Cubs, and I struck-out pinch-hitting against the Philadelphia Athletics' Howard Ehmke in Game One. I was traded in 1931 to the Cincinnati ball club, but I was shuffled off to Philadelphia where I ended my career in 1932.

Hack had an obsession about the dead ball being the cause for his decline, and I really don't know why he should think that, until I met him in 1948, shortly before he died from a fall he had at home. He was the lifeguard at the city pool in Baltimore, and I waved to him sitting up there in his high perch. He looked all tanned and healthy, until he climbed down off the tower and shook my hand. At least, I think he thought he was shaking my hand. You see, I died on January 19, 1939, in York, Pennsylvania, five days short of my 41st birthday. I was visiting Hack because I knew he would be joining us shortly, and I kind of wanted to clue him in on some of rules we have in the hereafter world.

"Hack, you're going to die next week from a fall, and then you'll be with us. Now, don't argue with me, you big lummox, because I'm the college boy in this picture. I heard you on the CBS radio show, and you sounded like you had some remorse about the mistakes you made, so that's why I'm here."

Hack had dark circles under his green eyes, and he also had several scars that I hadn't noticed before when we played together on the Cubbies. He must have thought he was having one of his deliriums because he didn't seem surprised when I told him I was dead. However, even this dead man's advice about keeping his nose clean and not getting angry about anything didn't seem to faze the old Hacker. He just stood there in his faded red swim suit and told me, "It was the ball, Heath. You know it's true, man, and I won't ever rest about that either. I could've made it out of my debt if they hadn't switched apples on us!"

I KIND OF LIVE A NICE life up in the territory above Earth. I rather picture it the way Mr. Wrigley must have seen it. He was always looking down at his boys playing on the field on Catalina Island, and I can also look down from where I am to watch the old club house on Catalina. See, there's an old ghost who still wanders in and out of that club house, and his name is Lewis Hack Wilson. The rules say that no baseball player can get up where I am until he rids himself of his baseball fever. I lost mine when I quit baseball and vacationed with my wife and two kids all over these United States. I died a happy man, with my wife and kids happy.

But old Hack, he died alone, and his own son wouldn't pick up the body. Ford Frick, the President of the National League, finally got Hack Wilson's body and buried him with his own money back in Martinsberg, West Virginia, where he began his baseball career. But, as they say, he still had the fever, because I can see him on foggy winter nights down below at the club house on Catalina Island. Mr. Cub, shortstop Ernie Banks, recently commemorated the plaque with famous Cubs on it, and he remarked that he felt a cold chill come over him. That was Hack.

I know what he's up to. He'll continue haunting that club house until he can find him one of those lively balls he thinks are stashed somewhere on the grounds. He wants me to come down to pitch to him once more, because old man Wrigley's mansion is still sitting on top of that hill waiting to be hit again, and I can see Hack's ghost looking up at me, with that grinning fool mug of his—that optimism that we survivors of the Great Depression have—waiting for just one more at bat to prove himself. I don't know if Hack will find his old goofy ball, but I'll keep an eye out for him. You can too, if you visit Catalina, and go through the Club House. Hell, maybe you can bring one of those magic balls and leave it there in the corner somewhere where Hack can find it. I'll keep listening for the glass to break up on Mt. Ada. When it does, I'll have a spot ready for Mr. Wilson.

The Somnambulist

HER HUSBAND, BILL, the pilot, calls her, and she agrees to have a reconciliation tryst on Catalina Island. She believes it will work out for the best. Her husband will retire to devote more time to her. They will be able to regain the emotional intimacy they once had before.

However, she looks down at the coffee table with the mirror top. She pictures herself leaning over the table, watching 25-year-old Stephen move upon her from behind, grabbing her shoulders and turning her toward him. He kisses her long and hard. As this image fills her consciousness, she makes another call. "Hi, Stephen? It's me. Let's do Catalina this weekend. Yes, I'm buying. Don't I always?"

As a former flight attendant, Eva is vivacious and seems to constantly attract those around her. Even at 42, her model looks have not faded, and men always look after her when she passes them, enjoying her slim figure and full breasts, which are bathed in the latest fashionable ensemble. She also wears dark purple eye shadow, as she loves horror, as the prospect of evil lurking all around her is a constant aphrodisiac to her mind. She is going to tell Stephen that it's over between them, and this will be their final meeting.

On the helicopter flight over from Long Beach, Eva tells Stephen she wants to turn on with him. "I think these magic mushrooms will help you overcome your fear of the unknown," she tells him. Eva knows that her boyfriend suffers from depression and night terrors, and he walks in his sleep. She has a strange feeling of motherly pity for him, even though they have been lovers for just a few months.

Stephen is a short man, about an inch shorter than Eva, but he is very handsome and muscular. He has dark hair and penetrating brown eyes. He also has a wit and sense of humor that attracted Eva to him from the first moment they met. She enjoys the fact that he's much younger and can sexually perform many more times than her middle-aged husband. Her husband also has no grasp of the absurd, and he is much more serious about life.

Stephen grasps her by the shoulders and speaks in a voice that is at once playful and profound. "Hey, I'm game. But this stuff won't fuck up my DNA or anything, will it? I don't want to become some zombie shuffling around watching the walls melt."

"No, but it will seriously alter your perception of life. I think you'll see how connected things are and how we all must learn to live in the here and now," she says.

As they walk up Crescent onto Metropole, Eva wants to share with Stephen some of the insights she has learned from her new psychedelic conversion. She is wearing a seashell necklace and blue bikini under a gauzy net sarong. Her sandals flap against the bottoms of her feet, and the ocean breezes caress her bronzed body as she leans against her lover. Stephen is pulling the large valise behind him, and he is wearing green and gray camouflage cargo shorts and a Pink Floyd tee that was a gift from Eva.

She has become much more aware of her surroundings, and she has also become more attentive to each moment in existence. "Look around you, Stephen. It's the eternal now that we're living. Religions tell us we must sacrifice ourselves for the unknowable future. What is that? A heaven of somebody's imagination? A hell where we all get punished for the sins, they tell us are unforgiveable? It's bullshit! All we have is right now. Billions of insects are crawling around in those hedges and between the cracks of this sidewalk. They all exist without a mythology of morality. They've existed for many more millions of years than we've been here, and they're still surviving. Where are we? We're on the brink of destroying ourselves with our weapons of mass destruction, our terrorism and our petty little lines drawn all over imaginary maps. Oh, you cross that line and I'll shoot you! Don't move next-door to me. You're the wrong color for this neighborhood. We just need to drop the bullshit divisions we've created and embrace our true nature."

Stephen has always respected Eva's intelligence. She has two years of college, and he is a college drop-out and unemployed fisherman. His parents divorced when he was born, and she comes from a family of seven that calls each other every day. He is having a difficult time understanding her, but he wants to get better. The nightmares and sleepwalking episodes are getting more frequent and dangerous. He found himself ten miles from his apartment in Coronado just two nights ago. He was wearing his underwear, and he didn't remember getting into the car. He had driven over the Coronado Bay Bridge into San Diego, and he had no recollection of it ever happening. The recurring nightmare he has is best described in a book he found in the library. He wonders how this artist from many years ago, named Lautréamont, could have the same vision that haunts his dreams. Maybe Eva is right. Maybe we all live in the same moment, and time is but a human invention to explain death.

As they come up to 229, Eva looks up at the façade of the building and smiles. "There it is, Stephen. The symbol of American ignorance." Across the portal in blue letters are the Spanish words "Casa Mariquita" on a sign with a pair of colorful Toucans. Beneath the sign, in redundant and ignorant splendor, is a blue canvas awning that says, "Casa Mariquita Hotel."

"Stephen, do you know what those words mean?" Eva asks.

"Nope," he says.

"They mean Ladybug House. Not Toucan House. The owners probably got the words from a Spanish dictionary and thought they sounded cute. You think they could at least look up the definition while they were inside the book. Or, worse yet, they knew what it meant, but they didn't want to use the image of a bug on their front porch sign. They think their customers are so stupid that they won't care about the name of the hotel and what it means."

Stephen squints up at the sign and begins nodding in agreement. "You're right. Who the hell do they think we are?"

Eva smiles. "Well, we're going to remedy that tonight. I've brought over a jar filled with ladybugs. And, at the exact stroke of midnight, I'm going to release them inside this hotel. Then, I'm going to knock on every door and recite the old children's rhyme about ladybugs."

"Hey, that's way cool!" Stephen says. "And I've got something I want to read to you about my bad dreams," he says.

"Good! See what I mean? You've already started to get the right attitude."

After checking in with a homely college student who wears tight red pants and speaks with a lisp, they go up to their room.

They have a partial ocean view, which means if you stick your head over the small balcony outside and stretch, you can see the water if you look through giant palm trees on the horizon. The bed is a King, with room to frolic, and there are two chairs around a small coffee table, with a clay flowerpot in the center containing some fresh red and white geraniums.

Stephen reaches over for a beer bottle on the nightstand. "Hey, do we have an opener?" he asks.

"Yes, go get the Swiss Army knife inside my handbag," says Eva, and Stephen gets up, walks over to the hand bag on the table and reaches into it. He pulls out the red knife with the white cross on it, and brings it over, pulling the can opener section from within the numerous tools contained inside the holder. He pops open the beer, closes the opener, and tosses the knife back into the open bag. He swigs from the bottle, hands it over to Eva, and she presses her lips against the perspiring neck, but she does not drink. Instead, she smiles over at her boyfriend and hands the bottle back to him, saying, "I don't do alcohol anymore, Stephen. It dulls the senses. I want to experience the total awareness of eternity."

One of his eyebrows rises in speculation, "That makes sense," he says. "Say, when are we going to take those mushrooms?"

"You, my dear, not we," says Eva. "One of us must be completely sober when this happens. I need to be aware so that you don't become too freaked out by what you'll see."

"Okay, but first I want to read you something," says Stephen, and he gets up from the bed, his testicles and penis swaying as he bends over his suitcase to slide open the zipper with his right hand. He then pulls out a paperback with a title on the cover that is printed in a circle and says, *Maldoror and the Complete Works of the Comte de Lautréamont.*

"I kept having this same nightmare, night after night, and I found this book in the Coronado City Library. It was a total accident, believe me. When I read you this passage, I want you to understand that I never read this book before I had my dream. I read this book after I kept having the dream. What this means is that this guy Lautréamont imagined my dream in the 1800s, and it came into my dreams in 2001." Stephen raises the book up to his face and reads:

"Now the swimmer and the female shark saved by him confront each other. For minutes they stare fixedly into each other's eyes. They swim circling, keeping each other in sight and each thinking: 'I was wrong all along. Here is one more evil than I.' Then in unison they glided underwater towards each other, in mutual admiration, the female shark slitting open the waves with her fins, Maldoror's arms thrashing the water; and they held their breaths, in deepest reverence, each one anxious to gaze for the first time upon his living image. Effortlessly, at only three yards apart, they suddenly fell upon one another like two magnets, in an embrace of dignity and gratitude, clasping each other tenderly as brother and sister. Carnal desire soon followed this display of affection. Like two leeches, a pair of nervous thighs gripped tightly against the monster's viscous flesh, and arms and fins wrapped around the objects of their desire, surrounding their bodies with love, while their breasts and bellies soon fused into one bluish-green mass reeking of sea-wreck, in the midst of the tempest still raging by the light of lightning; with the foamy waves for a wedding bed, borne on an undersea current as if in a cradle, rolling and rolling down into the bottomless ocean depths, they came together in a long, chaste, and hideous mating!... At last, I had found somebody who was like me!... From now on I was no longer alone in life... Her ideas were the same as mine... I was face to face with my first love!"

Eva sits for moment, digesting what she has just heard. She then decides something. She gets up from the bed, her breasts still glowing with sweat from their lovemaking, lifts up the sarong that is draped over the chair, and wraps it around her waist, and walks over to the hand bag sitting on the table. Finally, with a look of determination on her face, she thrusts her right hand down into the Hermes Birkin. She fumbles around for a moment and finally pulls out a zip-locked baggie containing the *Psilocybe semilanceata* or liberty cap psychedelic mushrooms.

She walks back over to the bed and sits on the edge, waving the baggie by her fingertips as if it is red hot and she's cooling it down. "This is what made Alice see her Wonderland. This is what will give you new eyes. But first, we go out to dinner and enjoy the world. I made reservations at the Avalon Grille. I have something I need to tell you."

Later that evening, when Eva tells Stephen that she is getting back together with her husband and she can't see him anymore, Stephen begins to eat more voraciously. The sixteen-ounce top sirloin disappears in five minutes, and he is smiling at her, as he leans back and lights a cigarette. "That was great, babe," he says and blows three smoke rings, the first a large one, the second a slightly smaller one that goes through the big one, and the third ring of smoke, even smaller, sails expertly through the second ring.

"Did you hear what I told you?" Eva asks.

"Sure, I hear you. I also heard what you told me earlier about the eternal now. That's what I'm doing. You and me. Right here and right now, baby," Stephen says.

"I'm glad you're being so mature about this, Stephen. That's why I've always been attracted to you, and I really want to help you. Let's go back to the hotel. It should be near midnight when we get there."

"Oh yeah. You're going to let loose the ladybugs. Cool."

Twenty minutes later, back in room 2, Eva is holding the big jar of ladybugs up to the wall light above the circular mahogany table. "I bought these beetles for twenty bucks online. There are two thousand in here," says Eva, staring at the crawling and flying insects inside the jar. Their wings are a polished red with black, irregular spots. They also have two white marks on either side of their heads and what look like white sclera and black pupils above their wriggling mandibles.

"So, what are they good for?" Stephen asks.

"I use them in my garden instead of insecticide. They can eat all the aphids and mites that destroy a garden, and then they move on," says Eva. "Pesticides are dangerous to man and beast, but these little darlings are natural garden angels."

"Okay, but what about the nursery rhyme? How does that go?"

"It's interesting. Farmers in England used the ladybugs to reduce the level of pests in their crops, and whenever they had to burn their fields after harvest, they chanted the rhyme in deference to what they called the ladybird. In America, we called them ladybugs because of the word's reference to a fire bug or pyromaniac," Eva smiles.

"Go ahead. Let me hear the rhyme," says Stephen.

It is now midnight. Eva stands up with her jar of ladybugs and regally walks over to the door. She opens it and carries the jar outside into the hallway. Stephen follows her. She unscrews the lid on the jar and shakes out the 2,000 beetles. Some of them land on the blue carpet; their red backs glow under the hall light like tiny fire engines.

Hundreds immediately open their wings and fly toward the hallway lights and even more sail out the open windows of the hacienda-like hotel. This is when Eva begins to knock on each of the hotel room doors. As she knocks, she recites the ladybug theme song, "Ladybug ladybug fly away home, your house is on fire and your children are gone, all except one and that's little Ann, for she crept under the frying pan."

As each occupied door opens, the resident looks out at the flying insects, listens to the woman singing her song, and either shuts the door immediately or smiles and asks what's happening.

"It's the Casa Mariquita!" says Eva. "The Ladybug House. We're celebrating ladybugs. They save vegetable gardens all over the world!" she laughs, and she and Stephen skip on down the hall to the next room.

Finally, after all the insects have disappeared, Eva and Stephen return to room 2 and shut the door behind them.

"Now we can release you from your bell jar, honey," says Eva.

"What bell jar?" Stephen asks.

"The great poetess, Sylvia Plath, wrote one novel about a girl who has mental problems. Like your bi-polar disorder. She believes she's living under a giant jar. This jar is her depression."

Eva picks up the baggie of mushrooms from the table, opens it, and takes out about three grams of dried fungi. "Here, Stephen, eat this. It'll taste kind of weird, but you can wash it down with some beer."

Stephen takes the mushrooms from her and stuffs them into his mouth, chews briefly, and then swallows. He makes a face but sits down on one of the chairs. He picks up his book and opens it to the page about his dream. "You know, this book is full of nightmares. He encourages readers to kidnap a child and torture it, to taste its tears and its blood—all within the first 30 pages. The author, Isidore Ducasse, was dead at 24. He believed men needed to become like animals and forget their human ways of religion and morals. He makes our Jim Morrison seem like he was in the Mickey Mouse Club."

"My, that's quite macabre. Let's play, Stephen, until you come on to the drug. It will blow your mind, young man, mark my words!"

The two lovers peel off their clothes and hop onto the bed. They play for almost an hour, when the psychedelic drug should be kicking in.

"Tell me what you see, Stephen," says Eva.

"What am I supposed to see?"

"Do the colors seem more vibrant? Do you see any new shapes or visions in the room?"

"No. Just you. You're the only vision I can see."

Eva seems perplexed. "I don't know. It should be working on you by now."

"Maybe you got some duds. It must happen sometimes. I'm tired. Let's call it a night, okay?"

Eva crawls under the covers and turns off the lamp on her side of the bed. "Goodnight, Stephen. I'm sorry about the drug. I suppose it may not work on certain people. I've enjoyed today. I really have. We were wonderful together, and I'm sure you'll find somebody soon who can make you happy."

In the darkness, Stephen stares up at the ceiling. He sees a multi-colored ball as it begins to circle in the air, radiating streams of light, like one of those big balls hanging above the dance floors at the discothèques of the 80s. He falls asleep thinking about a world where animals rule over all of us.

Inside his mind, Stephen awakens to the sound of water. It is the ocean; the booming waves of the Pacific are crashing against the hull of his fishing boat. Stephen feels immediately panicked. He is at sea, and his heart races as he stares around in the darkness. He reaches over and turns on the light above him on his cabin's bulkhead. What greets him defies logic. Beside him in the bed is a giant shark! How did you get in here? He can feel the ocean beneath him, colliding with the hull and sending vibrating rivulets all along his rack. It's my job. I must do it.

He gets up from the bed and fumbles around the room. He picks up the flowerpot from the table and brings it over to the bed. He looks down at the shark in the bed. It is still alive! He can see its deathly eyes and those gills behind them are moving in and out! He raises the flowerpot high above his head and then brings it crashing down onto the head of the shark. The shark begins twisting and flopping in the bed, snapping its razor-sharp teeth at Stephen's legs. You demon! I'll kill you!

Stephen lunges toward the handbag on the table, thinking it's his sea bag. He hears a scream somewhere in the distance. Maybe it's Elliott playing his damned Heavy Metal again. He finds the knife. He pulls out the longest blade and lunges over the bed toward the shark. The shark tries to break his arm with its jaws, but Stephen acts quickly, just the way he always does at these moments. He straddles the giant monster's back, with his left hand holding onto the black dorsal fin. Expertly, like a deft surgeon of the sea, Stephen plunges the knife's blade deep inside the back of the shark to sever the spinal column and put an end to the heartless beast of the ocean.

JULY 23, 2012, AVALON, Catalina Island.

The Catalina Island Ghost Tour is walking down Metropole. The sun has already set, and the streets are darkly shrouded with gloomy shadows. Island residents and tourists who know about the tour make sarcastic comments and noises at the people who are wearing the glowing necklaces. The residents think the tour casts an unfavorable light into the hidden dark places on Catalina, and so they make derogatory moans and screams, hoping to show what a phony deal this tour is.

However, the tour members seem to be up for it. They follow their guide until he stops them in front of the Casa Mariquita Hotel. He points to the hotel, and the tourists stop talking to listen to him.

"Before I take you down the alley across the street, the same alley that 25-year-old Stephen Otto Reitz used to walk to the Catalina Fire Station on the night he reported the death of his girlfriend, 42-year-old Eva Marie Weinfurtner, I want you to know about what residents of the hotel have experienced following this death in room 2. Some who have stayed in the same room have reported blood coming up from the carpet. Others said they heard the sounds of the ocean and screams. One person even said she heard someone singing the old nursery rhyme about Ladybugs flying away home. Who knows? I do believe that when humans die by foul means, their spirits often come back to inhabit the place where they died. Could that be the case with Eva Marie? She was a beautiful cougar."

The guide holds up a photograph of Eva taken from the newspapers reporting her death in 2001. "She was just about to get back with her pilot husband, but she wanted just one more weekend with her young lover. What makes this death intriguing is the fact that young Stephen Reitz was a sleepwalker and a man who suffered from bi-polar mental problems. His parents said they rigged alarms all over the house to warn them when Stephen was walking in his sleep. He would often drive and journey long distances, never remembering his trip after he awoke. On the night of the death of Mrs. Weinfurtner, Stephen said he awoke from a deep sleep, and he saw the body of his lover slumped over in the bed. When he saw that her spine had been punctured, he had a moment of déjà vu. He was a commercial fisherman, and he had used this method to kill many large fish and sharks. However, as he told the firemen at the station that night, he had no memory of killing her. All he remembered was having a dream about fighting off an intruder. He said he was completely unconscious when he killed his girlfriend. The jury at his trial, however, did not buy his story. The force of the blows to the head and the use of the knife would have taken more strength than a sleeping person could exert. Therefore, Stephen is today serving a 26-years-to-life prison term for the murder of Eva Marie Weinfurtner."

"Maybe he thought she was a shark!" says a young girl standing in the front row of the tourists.

The tour guide laughs. "Well, now that's an interesting theory. If that were the case, then perhaps Stephen changed his dream's antagonist because he thought his story was too crazy to believe. He did admit that he knew how to kill by severing the spinal cord, and that's what he did to poor Eva. I guess only his mind will know for certain. Either way, poor Eva is dead and still haunting the Casa Mariquita. By the way, is anybody staying there?" the tour guide asks.

A Hispanic man and his woman sheepishly raise their hands.

"Room 2?" the guide asks.

"No, we're in room 6," says the young man, and his girlfriend or wife grips his hand tighter.

"Well, let us know if you see or hear anything strange. We're up on the Web and on Facebook. You can upload any photos there. I'm certain Eva Marie would be dying to see them," the guide smiles, and he turns to begin the walk across the street and down the alley toward the fire station.

As the tour group walks down the alley, the same little girl who asked the question about the shark looks up at her father and asks, "Daddy, if that lady can be a cougar, then why can't she be a shark, too?"

Her father laughs and lifts her up into his strong arms. "You're right, Jenna! Who knows what we see? The light from the universe comes into our eyes and whatever our brain sees, that's what it believes. A guy named Trotsky, who was killed in Mexico by an assassin with an icepick, once said, 'Everything is relative in this world, where change alone endures.' The here and now, I suppose, is only limited by our own imaginations."

Kafka and the Chewing Gum Man

THE SPIRIT OF FRANZ Kafka is known in the world of the mystical beings as "the joker." In his life, he was the author of surrealistic and dark stories that were difficult to interpret. For example, a young man awakens one morning and discovers he has changed into a bug. Not "like" a bug, mind you, but an actual bug. The rest of the story continues from his perspective, as he is held prisoner inside his own family's home, and he eventually dies from an apple lodged in his back, which his sister throws at him in frustration.

Kafka's ghost believes that he can change another spirit's existential predicament by altering or metamorphosing that person's reality in the spirit world. Since the goal of all ghosts in the spirit world is to go beyond our worldly plane of existence and meld into the great Oneness of Being, Kafka serves a beneficial purpose. Let's join him now as he confronts perhaps his biggest challenge yet on Catalina Island.

William Wrigley Junior refused to print a comma after his last name. He said it was because he never wanted to forget that it was his father who gave him the chance to learn how to succeed in business. Of course, Franz Kafka's father was a tyrannical businessman, and his son never wanted to even attempt being as unscrupulous as his father was. Wrigley and Kafka were like fire and ice meeting in the hereafter. Whereas Kafka was an excellent student and eventually became a lawyer in his hometown of Prague, Wrigley was expelled from school in Philadelphia, and his father gave him the most difficult job in his soap factory to try to straighten him out. Wrigley Junior stirred the giant pots of soap with a huge paddle, and it made him physically strong. William Jr. maintained that strength his entire life by exercising and playing sports. He especially loved baseball, and when he made a success of his own business, selling chewing gum, one of the first items on his agenda was to purchase an interest in the Chicago Cubs in 1916 and a controlling interest in 1921.

So it is that the joker, Franz Kafka, a master of the absurd, meets one of the most successful businessmen in the history of America on an island off the coast of Southern California. William has just left his body, which is interred inside his memorial, a 130 feet tall tower that stands above a botanical garden in the valley below. This memorial is at the end of Avalon Canyon Road, and Kafka can see Wrigley's form as Kafka walks toward him. Franz stops and stands next to an endemic Lemonade Berry plant. Of course, the two ghosts are ephemeral and transparent, and the dignitaries from the material world, who are climbing up to the memorial to pay their last respects, are oblivious to both figures.

"Welcome to the afterlife, Mister Wrigley," says Kafka, the hint of a smile on his dark-complexioned face. Franz is thin, with neatly parted black hair, and he wears a suit he wore to his job every day at the insurance company. It is double-breasted, and his tie is from the wide variety available in the early part of the twentieth century. In human terms, it is 1932, but in the spirit world there is no time other than the time it takes to do the deed you must perform to transcend.

Wrigley looks pale and startled in his charcoal gray herringbone suit and tie and starched, high-collared white shirt. His face is handsome, with a cleft in his chin and his oiled hair is wavy and cut short. Even in death he has a smile for his new host. "You know me? I'm afraid I haven't had the pleasure, Mister...?"

"Just call me K. I suppose you're wondering why you can walk through these people and objects. Don't be amazed. You're now part of the world that I only discovered late in my own life, as I lay dying from tuberculosis. My youth, I am sad to say, was spent disavowing any type of spirit world. However, it is, as they say, never too late to become aware of the eternal light, or *ein sof*, as my people call it."

"I can't assume these things, my good fellow. I am a practical realist. If what I see is real, then so be it. I will adapt. Just as I adapted all my life to the fluctuations of the economy and the principles of capitalism." Wrigley attempts to shake Kafka's hand, but he is still too new as a spirit to have any substance, and his large hand goes right through Kafka's smaller hand.

"Don't worry. After I show you around, you'll be able to feel the spirit world as you felt your old world of material reality. However, to do this, you must first pass a bit of a test." Kafka does his best imitation of a man swinging a baseball bat. He also takes out a stick of Spearmint gum from his top pocket, folds it carefully, and inserts it into his mouth. As he begins to chew, he chuckles.

"What are you laughing at, young man?" says Wrigley, frowning. "And you say I must compete? Compete for what? What use is there for me in this world where I cannot live through my senses?"

"Let me ask you a question. Did you ever once consider that your materialistic view of the world was absurd?" Kafka asks.

"Absurd? I don't understand your meaning. Are you presuming my career was without any meaning?" Wrigley says.

"Yes, absurd. I spent my career attempting to show the world that they lived an absurd existence. However, now that I am here, it is my job to show people like you how to understand how your life can be seen from an entirely different perspective. Naturally, when one is successful, such as yourself, life seems to be dynamic and full of material wealth. You view the world like your monument up there on the hill. You are substantial and high above everything, daring someone to knock you over. However, did you know, they are going to move your body from this monument because they're afraid it will be harmed by the Japanese, who will have attacked an island in the Hawaiian chain, and your family will be afraid they will travel on to attack Catalina and the California coast? Your family is afraid for your body, even though you are here, with me, trying to understand why life in their world is absurd."

"You're a strange bird," says Wrigley, sizing up Kafka as he walks around him. "What are you going to show me about this world that I loved so much? I made thousands of jobs for my fellow Americans, and I saved this island from certain ruin through the largesse of my earnings! What do I have to learn about your absurdity?"

"First of all, seeing how absurd life is requires a change in perspective." Kafka walks over to Wrigley and puts his hand on his head. "Right now, we're going to go to visit the forests of Meso-america, in the state of Quintana Roo, where your chicle is harvested. You have never visited this place because your industrial managers were given that job. You were the salesman who taught America to love chewing gum, and this part of the enterprise was never important to you unless the supply wasn't fast enough to make you wealthy."

After Kafka's touch, both spirits are transported instantly to the jungles of Quintana Roo. Around them, the chicleros are climbing the sapodilla trees, making zigzagging gouges in the bark as they slide down each tree. "The latex runs down the tree to protect it, but these extractors need to harvest this substance to fill the mouths of your chewing cows in America! Want to feel what it's like?" says Kafka.

The spirit of William Wrigley condenses into a point of light and then it explodes, shooting across the jungle, entering a giant sapodilla as it's being cut. Wrigley sees the machete as it comes down hard on his skin, slicing across his soft bark like a warrior's sword, and the confectionary magnate can feel pain for the first time in his new existence. He cannot scream out, however, as trees have no method of agony, so he must endure the excruciating cuts. He can feel the chiclero work his way down the surface.

He is a Maya, and he wears loose gabardine and a red wool cap, and his lithe body hangs back on the rope wrapped around the girth of the tree. He moves down again, slicing his zigzag pattern, talking to the sapodilla as he slides down from the great heights in the canopy of the rain forest. "*Tzicte'ya'*, my wounded noble tree. You give my family life. I will mark you with this special sign, so I will know to come back in five years. You must provide your tears to me once more, noble tree!" Wrigley's spirit can feel the streams of latex as they drip in wavy patterns down the length of his trunk. The men at the bottom collect this latex, process it, and roll it into giant balls to be inserted into wooden containers for transport.

"Come back!" says Kafka, and Wrigley's ghost instantly exits the tree and streaks across the jungle paths until he stands in his human form once more next to his guide. However, Wrigley's suit is now torn to shreds, and his face is gauged with zigzag scars.

"The scars never leave the tree, my friend," says Kafka. "They are scarred for life, as you are also marked now that you've experienced life as a tree."

Wrigley looks shaken, but he is still belligerent. "What the hell does this prove? Men are not trees. We use Nature for our own devices. It says so in the Bible. We name everything, and we use everything."

Kafka smiles. "Oh, but we in the spirit world are allowed the gift of hindsight and foresight. We can travel, like the Mayans say, through space and time and into eternal paradise itself. Don't you want to be in the authentic Paradise, Mister Wrigley?"

Wrigley stomps his foot. "If this is your idea of paradise, then no, I don't. What are you up to, young man? I must admit, I never expected to be part of such a fantastic world."

"Your company paid these workers very little. They had to buy all their food, clothing and supplies out of their wages from the company store, so the nature of the industry produced smugglers and pirates who would raid the camps, kill the workers, and steal their chicle. You didn't care where you got your latex, however, so what problem was it for you, right?" Kafka again touches the shoulder of the executive, and they are instantly transported into the future, 1944, on the battlefield of Italy, near the Benedictine Monte Cassino Catholic Monastery.

The Americans are attacking the Nazis, who are scattered all over the hill beneath the monastery, in groups of machine gun nests and heavy artillery placements. Shells rain down over the land and explode in plumes of dirt, debris, and human limbs. Men scream out in pain as they are hit by shrapnel and bullets digging into their bodies like the scarification of the sapodilla trees.

"The Allies have fought for three months against these German forces. They fight each other, and land and religion get in the way. There are reports that the church abbey, there since the year 529, is being used by the Germans to spot the artillery shelling. There is a debate in the press about it. One general says, 'If the abbey's not being used now, it will be used by the enemy in the future.' The result is what you will see now. But first, look at these men. See? They are all chewing your gum, Mister Wrigley! See that young soldier over there lying on his back in the road? As he bleeds and dies, he still chews the product of your enterprise. Is he getting satisfaction? Does the flavor last until his last breath? You got the contract! At least, your son Philip did. He was a good businessman, Mister Wrigley, just like his father. Every soldier has a ration of chewing gum in his war kit of personal objects, along with c-rations and soap. Aren't you feeling proud right now?"

The bombers then came from out of the east, growling and dropping their payloads on this historic holy site of antiquity. Thousands of bombs are falling, destroying the colorful tapestries and frescoes hanging on the walls, exploding the giant crucifix and golden altar where monks have held their masses for hundreds of years. Objects of worth, historical antiques of religious worship, and the people living inside, who are not German soldiers, are all destroyed by these Allied bombs.

"If war is not the supreme act of absurdity, then I really don't know what is," says Kafka. "While you can manufacture chewing gum and make millions of dollars, there are Mayans who die in the jungles of Mexico, Belize and Guatemala, so these brave soldiers can chew their last flavored Spearmint or Juicy Fruit piece, while the bombs explode to hell a religious shrine of the people."

William Wrigley at last seems to break. His face contorts into a wrinkled grimace, and tears stream down his handsome cheeks, and his spirit body shudders. "Stop it! I've seen enough! Take me back to Catalina. I want to rest in peace."

"No, there is one more absurdity I want you to see, and it's a magnificent one. In fact, if you can learn from it, then I think you'll be on your way to evolutionary change." Kafka once more touches the older man on his shoulder, and they both disappear.

They are standing in the freezing cold center of Chicago's South Side. The population is mostly Black, and this could even be 1931, if it weren't for the kids with iPod cords and cell phones glued to their ears and thrust in front of their bodies as they stroll around the streets, texting and laughing in a forced, high-pitched banter that expresses the abnormal tension in the winter air.

There are the gangsters working in the shadows of car doors in the middle of the neighborhood's dead-end streets with dirty snow piled up in the corners. Some are even from Mexico, part of the new threat that causes more deaths of young people every day than the international wars in Iraq and Afghanistan combined. Guns are sold from the trunks of these low-riding vehicles that spit out booming hip-hop with their angry words, along with the free tastes of marijuana, zip-locked in plastic baggies, fresh from the American and Mexican rural government lands and state parks that go unattended because of federal and state cutbacks.

Kafka's ghost points to a billboard above the bus stop bench where they are standing. The ad shows a lovely young woman with long hair, with her mouth open wide, exposing the circular metal cover for a sewer. On this cover it says "City" in engraved letters. The lettering at the bottom right of the ad says: Dirty mouth? Nothing cleans it up like Orbit.

Kafka says, "Your company now sells that brand again. In 1944, it was introduced to the people as a replacement for your other brands, which were all shipped to the fighting men overseas. Today, it is sold again with ads like these."

Wrigley smiles. "Yes, I can see Philip doing something like that. I taught him all I know. It's advertising that sells, Mister K. I came to this city with $50. I sold soap with gum, and when people liked the gum better than the soap, I switched to selling gum. I gave them a fresh, kissing sweet mouth. I mailed free gum to everybody in the phone books in major cities right after the stock market crashed. It worked! My company became rich because I sold people what they wanted. By God, I cleaned their teeth and made them smile in the middle of their troubles, and I'm proud of that!"

"It isn't your son, Philip, who owns your company now. Or did own your company, I should say. First, your grandson, William Wrigley Junior owned it until he died in 1999 at age 66. Your company had two billion dollars in sales. Today is January 22, 2010, and your great-grandson, your namesake, William Wrigley Jr. has just sold the company you founded."

Wrigley looks shocked. "What? He sold my company?"

"Yes, and your baseball team was sold earlier, too. Today, family owners are selling out to the giant conglomerates, like Mars Incorporated, and leaving business forever. He was able to retire with twenty-three billion dollars in his pocket," says Kafka.

"Retire? He left all those workers with families to feed. He left the excitement of business and sales. What kind of son is he?" cries Wrigley, as a young Black teen in a down jacket runs after another young man, and they both pass through the ephemeral bodies of K. and W.

"Did you know there are new entrepreneurs who have taken up your sales gimmicks?" asks Kafka. "Look over there. See that young dealer selling his baggie of marijuana to that even younger customer? He has put a box of Orbit gum in with his merchandise. He knows the weed dries out the mouth, so he's giving away your gum to help the user prevent his cotton mouth."

"What? Are you equating that criminal with my enterprise? You're insane! I followed the law. I was an honorable Republican and prohibitionist. I didn't allow tobacco or liquor in my club house with the Cubs."

"I'm afraid it's all relative, Mister Wrigley. Business, after all, is business. Did you ever stop to think of the dark side of your own enterprise? No, probably not. Well, the ancients in

Mesoamerica did. While they were scaling your sapodilla trees to make a quick profit, they were also planting their maize, beans, and squash, without pesticides and fertilizers, in order to balance out Nature. However, in the wealthy North Americas, we create consumers of everything imaginable. Businessmen are today injecting animals with dangerous hormones to make them fat sooner, so these businesses can profit from these plump creatures on our dinner tables and in our fast-food enterprises. Many vegetables, like corn, and your gum, are being synthetically manipulated in a laboratory, causing permanent genetic damage that can eventually cause world shortages of these same vegetables. And drugs? Well, my friend, I am afraid the world's drug salesmen are making quite a bit more than your chewing gum. Mexican drug cartels are making over sixty-five billion dollars a year on sales in the North Americas alone. That's quite a bit more than chewing gum, my chum."

"I can't be responsible for all this! How does my business even begin to compare with what you're telling me?" Wrigley's voice sounds frightened.

"During the Great Depression, people chewed your gum, but they also got ulcers because your gum created acid in their stomachs because your customers didn't eat regularly. Little boys put gum on the bottoms of school chairs and movie seats, causing extra work for custodians and janitors. They even threw their used gum in the street where other people would step on it and cause a sticky crisis on the way to an important business appointment. It got into people's hair; it stuck to dentures; it caused entire economies in Mesoamerica to rise and fall! Your gum is not a drug, thank goodness, but it does have its dark side."

Kafka turns toward Wrigley, who is staring off into the distance, as if he wants to escape.

"Let's go one more place, Mister Wrigley. I want you to see the world from a different, more magical perspective. I believe you need this now."

Kafka puts his hand on Wrigley's head, and they both disappear in a puff of glittering particles of spirit matter.

It is December 21, 2012. They are both standing beneath the warm sun, in a crowded street of downtown Mexico City. The traffic around them is congested, with smoke, honking horns, and Spanish obscenities being shouted, circulating around them like a fanatical symphony of anger.

However, in a far corner of the street, next to a Catholic Church, a band of Mayans watches the sky from the shadows of their vegetable stand. They are selling the fresh produce from their milpas, the perfect balancing act of two years of cultivation and eight years of letting the area lay fallow. There is no more harvesting of chicle, as it has been replaced by synthetic latex from the laboratories. However, this day on the Mayan Calendar marks a turning point in the universal evolution of creation and destruction.

As both Wrigley and Kafka watch, transfixed, the living natives slowly turn into spiritual beings, their flesh becoming transparent, and their bodies shine amid all the pollution and modern machinery of the age. They stare up at the sky, and it opens to them. Nobody else but the spirit world can see that an ancient prophesy is being fulfilled.

A long cleft spreads out across the multi-colored tapestry of the heavens until a pattern of woven serpent ropes is seen, flattened out, with long tentacles hanging down, ever descending to the earth. Realty, in essence, has become undergirded by this system of threadlike links. In other words, space-time itself is woven together in ways that human beings, stuck within the three-dimensional space-time fabric of observable reality, cannot really perceive. Only the Mayan spirit-beings and all the other worldly spirits, like Kafka and Wrigley, can see what reality is.

"What does it mean for a serpent cord to descend and open? Who is traveling through the hole in space-time? Is this a fanciful fairy tale, Mister Wrigley? Or is this your new reality?" Kafka, for a final time, puts his hand on the shoulder of the great industrialist.

"This is where we are born and where we go when we learn enough from our life to warrant an escape," says Wrigley, and he looks down at his hands. They are now less transparent, and they can feel the fabric of his suit as he presses them against his chest.

"Yes, this is where the prophets and the holy beings go up and down to be born and reborn. It is a form of Jacob's Ladder, where the angels travel to their celestial paradise. You have learned a lot in a short time, Mister Wrigley. I think you might just learn to evolve here." Franz Kafka reaches out and he shakes the hand of the recent spirit-being, and William Wrigley Jr. thrusts his head back and he laughs uproariously, as the sound of his glee travels out to the serpent ropes, which the Mayans are now climbing, so they can finally be with their Maker. Around him, the spirits of Philip Wrigley and William Wrigley Jr. walk toward him, smiles on their ghostly faces, chewing their gum, wanting to shake the hand of their founding father, who has, at long last, come home.

I've been in a Bram Stoker Finalist anthology, and I've won the First Place Blue Ribbon for Best Historical Mystery, *Forevermore*, at the Chanticleer International Book Awards. My literary short story, *Jasmine*, is in the upcoming short fiction anthology *Call Down the Moon* published by Propertius Press on August 22, 2022. My most recent horror publication, *Cousins*, is in the upcoming anthology *Edgar Allan Poe Time Traveler*, published by Pro Se Productions. My story *Bug Motel* is the lead story in the HellBound Books horror anthology, *Toilet Zone 3*. My adult short fiction anthology *Valley of the Dogs, Dark Stories*, won the Silver Medal at the 2021 Reader's Favorite international contest. My two historical mystery series are published through and curated by the American Library Association's Biblioboard.com. I have an M.A. Degree in Creative Writing from San Diego State University.

Author James Musgrave

Don't miss out!

Visit the website below and you can sign up to receive emails whenever Jim Musgrave publishes a new book. There's no charge and no obligation.

https://books2read.com/r/B-A-UBZT-WSPZB

BOOKS 2 READ

Connecting independent readers to independent writers.

Did you love *Catalina Ghost Stories*? Then you should read *Valley of the Dogs, Dark Stories*[1] by James Musgrave!

[2]

Dark Stories for Readers with Surreal and Deep Tastes

Silver Medal Winner of the 2021 Reader's Favorite International Contest for Best Adult Anthology

A B.R.A.G.Medallion Honoree, 2021

9.25 overall Evaluation at BookLife, *Publishers Weekly*

Hollywood and Broadway are icons of the American Dream. But what happens to those who feed off that dream? Just as drug cartels have many underlings, who must get paid along the journey to the addicts, so do the characters who need to

---

1. https://books2read.com/u/bPy5Rd

2. https://books2read.com/u/bPy5Rd

be nourished by the luminaries who make up this star-studded world above us. James Musgrave's collection of eleven stories, in many ways, addresses the theme of "star power," but in a way that satirizes the stereotypical "Hollywood endings" in very unique and literary ways. This collection has a remedy for the past year's traumas caused by a worldwide pandemic.

Award-winning short fiction author, Jacob M. Appel says, "With the publication of Valley of the Dogs, Jim Musgrave joins the ranks of George Saunders, Steven Millhauser, and Kevin Brockmeier at the heart of the modern American short story's second great renaissance."

"Entering the consciousness of a reader is the most sacred enterprise an author can have. These stories have been collected as my Zen reflection during the past year's COVID-19 plague. This shamanistic mental state, which the Japanese term "Mushin," or "no-mind" is close to the stream-of-consciousness technique that Henry James, Virginia Woolf, Jack Kerouac, James Joyce, and William Faulkner used to such success. However, it is also a form of channeling that defies definition. This is the mystical realm that creatives around the world know so well, and we worship at its altar every day we put fingers to keys or pen to paper. I want to thank readers who enjoy dark stories, as in this age of political correctness and what publishers often term "accessibility," it is becoming more difficult for us authors, especially us authors who don't make a lot of money from our work, to find an audience. I will go out on a limb and say that if the author does make a lot of money from a dark story, he/she will get marketing to back him/her up to ride the tide of money to the bank. If you ride this wave of Gustav and all the other characters in my collection, then thanks for that. It's been a tough year for all of us. Bless you." --James Musgrave

"If you only read the books that everyone else is reading, you can only think what everyone else is thinking."

— Haruki Murakami, Norwegian Wood

Hey, my "sore loser" book VALLEY OF THE DOGS DARK STORIES is up on B&N's website. See what a sore loser writes! This author is completely banned forever at the exotic and reputable folks at the Poohbah SELF-PUBLISHED BOOK AWARDS (COPYRIGHT SERVICE).

So, it's now "officially" a "banned book"! Cool beans!

Read more at https://emrepublishing.com.